CATHRYN
FALWELL

Mystery
Vine

A Pumpkin Surprise

Greenwillow Books
An Imprint of HarperCollinsPublishers

Mystery Vine: A Pumpkin Surprise
Copyright © 2009 by Cathryn Falwell
All rights reserved. Manufactured in China.
For information address HarperCollins Children's Books,
a division of HarperCollins Publishers,
10 East 53rd Street, New York, NY 10022.
www.harpercollinschildrens.com

Collages were used to prepare the full-color art.
The text type is Garamond.

Library of Congress Cataloging-in-Publication Data

Falwell, Cathryn.
Mystery vine: a pumpkin surprise / by Cathryn Falwell.
p. cm.
"Greenwillow Books."
Summary: When a mysterious vine appears in their carefully tended garden,
the brother and sister patiently watch and wait to see what it becomes.
Includes gardening activities and pumpkin recipes.
ISBN 978-0-06-177198-9 (trade bdg.) — ISBN 978-0-06-177197-2 (lib. bdg.)
[1. Stories in rhyme. 2. Gardens—Fiction. 3. Plants—Fiction. 4. Vegetables—Fiction.
5. Brothers and sisters—Fiction.] I. Title.
PZ8.3.F2163My 2009 [E]—dc22 2008043437

09 10 11 12 13 [SCP] First Edition 10 9 8 7 6 5 4 3 2 1
Greenwillow Books

For my creative brothers—
Douglas, a champion pumpkin carver,
&
David, a green-thumb gardener—
and for Bailey, my tomato hound

Last spring we planted
lots of seeds.
We watched them grow,
and pulled the weeds.

First came lettuce,
crisp and crunching.
Bright green peas,
so good for munching.

Radishes all in a line . . .
But what was that
young Mystery Vine?

With sunny days and
summer showers,
tomato plants made
tiny flowers.
We tied the beans
to poles with twine,
and watched the creeping
Mystery Vine.

The vine grew on,
and overnight
came yellow blossoms,
big and bright.

Carrot tops were
good for tickles;
cucumbers, for
making pickles.
We looked and looked
for clue or sign
to help us guess
the Mystery Vine.

Then we found other
things to do,
but the Mystery Vine
still grew and grew.

Fall is here.

It's getting cold.

The garden now

is looking old.

But look!

Surprise!
The Mystery Vine
is growing pumpkins,
round and fine!

Lots of pumpkins!
Big and small.
Lots of pumpkins!
Short and tall.
Pumpkin breads
and pies to eat.

Jack-o'-lanterns!

Trick or treat!

We toast the seeds,
but I save mine . . .
to plant another
Mystery Vine!

PUMPKIN RECIPES

ROASTED PUMPKIN SEEDS

Pumpkin seeds are a tasty and healthy snack, and they are easy to roast.

Ingredients
1 tablespoon of canola or olive oil
1 teaspoon of salt
1 pumpkin

Supplies
1 colander
1 large bowl
1 sheet-cake pan

1. Preheat the oven to 300 degrees.

2. Scoop out the pumpkin and separate the seeds from the pulp. Put the seeds in a colander and rinse them well under cold water. Pat them dry with a towel.

3. Mix about 2 cups of seeds with the oil and salt in a large bowl.

4. Pour the seeds onto a sheet-cake pan and spread them out in a single layer.

5. Roast them in the oven for about 30 minutes, stirring every 5–10 minutes. Watch carefully, so they don't burn.

6. Seeds are done when they are crunchy and a light golden brown. If the husks are chewy, just eat the soft and nutty insides.

Always have an adult with you when you cook, especially when using an oven. Use oven mitts or hot pads when moving pans in and out of the oven. Also note that oven temperatures may vary. It won't hurt to check the pumpkin bread loaves at 40 minutes (see next page) and then put them back in the oven if they're not done.

PUMPKIN APPLE BREAD

This recipe makes three small loaves: one to share, one to freeze for later, and one to enjoy yourself! Or you can make one large loaf—just bake it for 50–60 minutes.

Ingredients

1½ cups flour (plus a bit for dusting your pans)

1 teaspoon baking soda

½ teaspoon baking powder

½ teaspoon salt

½ teaspoon cinnamon

½ teaspoon nutmeg

½ teaspoon ground cloves

2 large eggs (beaten lightly)

½ cup canola oil

1½ cups sugar

1 cup cooked or canned pumpkin

1 tart apple (a Granny Smith is a good choice)

¼ cup water

Supplies

2 large bowls

3 small bread pans (3˝ x 5˝)

1 toothpick

cooling racks

1. Preheat the oven to 350 degrees.

2. Grease and lightly flour all three bread pans.

3. Combine the flour, baking soda, baking powder, salt, cinnamon, nutmeg, and ground cloves in one of the bowls.

4. Mix the eggs, oil, sugar, pumpkin, and water in the other bowl. Stir well.

5. Gradually pour the liquid ingredients into the dry ingredients. Stir just until mixed together.

6. Now peel and chop the apple into small cubes. You will need about one cup. (If your apple is very large, you can eat the extra!)

7. Gently stir the apple pieces into the batter, then spoon the batter into the prepared pans.

8. Bake for 40–50 minutes, until a toothpick inserted into the center comes out clean.

9. Cool the pans on a rack for 10 minutes, then remove the loaves from the pans to finish cooling.

GARDENING FUN

FUNNY FACES

Make an egg friend who will grow green hair!

Materials

1 raw egg

⅓ cup of potting soil*

a pinch of seeds, such as wheat grass, alfalfa, rye, radish, or birdseed mix

1 permanent marker

1 small jar lid or bottle cap

1. Carefully crack the top off a raw egg so that ¾ of the shell is left. (Save the inside of the egg to cook later.)

2. Rinse out the shell and fill it with potting soil.

3. Sprinkle a small amount of water on the soil, and gently press it down a little bit.

4. Sprinkle the seeds on top, and then add a little more soil to cover the seeds.

5. Use the marker to make a face on the shell. Be careful! Eggshells are very fragile.

6. Place the egg-head planter in the lid so that it doesn't roll around, and find a warm, safe place for it.

7. Give it a few drops of water every day—just enough to keep the soil damp.

8. In a week or so, your funny-face egg head will grow "hair" from the seeds!

*If you don't have potting soil, you can use a couple of cotton balls instead. Just dampen them a bit before putting them into the eggshell, and sprinkle the seeds on top.

BE A PLANT SPY

See how a seed becomes a plant!

Materials

1 clear, empty glass jar
some seeds: dried beans, peas, or corn
1 paper towel
1 sheet of old newspaper

1. Fold up a paper towel, dampen it, and press it against the inside of the jar.

2. Slide the seeds between the paper towel and the glass. Fill the rest of the jar with some bunched-up newspaper.

3. Keep the jar out of direct sunlight and keep the paper towel damp.

4. In a few days you will see tiny roots poke out of the seeds, and soon a plant stem will reach up toward the top of the jar.

5. When the stems and leaves poke over the edge, move the jar to a sunny window. Keep the paper towel damp, and watch the plants grow!

Other Growing Ideas

If you don't have a place for a vegetable garden, try some of these ideas:

- Grow plants on a porch, patio, or balcony. Big pots, barrels, or other large containers can hold tomatoes, herbs, lettuce, or even Mystery Vines!

- Place the pointy end of a sweet potato in a jar of water. Use toothpicks to help hold half the potato above the rim. Now watch! Roots grow down, and vines grow up!

- Poke a small hole in the bottom of an empty yogurt cup, then fill it with potting soil. Plant seeds from the fruits and vegetables you get at the grocery store—lemons, grapefruits, apples, tomatoes, or others. See what will grow!

Happy gardening!

MAKE A BOOK VINE

See how long
you can grow your vine!

Materials

colored paper
a long piece of thick yarn
markers, crayons, or colored pencils

1. Use colored paper to make leaf shapes.

2. Each time you read a book, write the title on a leaf.

3. Tape the leaves to the yarn to make the vine grow.
   You can add pumpkins, too!

Happy reading!

Blueberries for Sal

A Chair for My Mother

Turtle Splash!

Feast for 10

The Carrot Seed

The Runaway Bunny